the ChimpanSNEEZE

P9-CEZ-357

For the Kuta Family,

MEG, DAVE, and HIP-HIP-HOORACHEL

—A.Z.

No part of this publication may be reproduced, stored in a retrieval system,
or transmitted in any form or by any means, electronic, mechanical, photocopying,
recording, or otherwise, without written permission of the publisher.
For information regarding permission, write to Scholastic Inc.,
Attention: Permissions Department, 557 Broadway, New York, NY 10012.

ISBN 978-0-545-39870-1

Copyright © 2012 by Aaron Zenz

All rights reserved. Published by Scholastic Inc.
SCHOLASTIC and associated logos are trademarks
and/or registered trademarks of Scholastic Inc.

12 11 10 9 8 7 6 5 4 3 2 1   12 13 14 15 16 17/0

Printed in the U.S.A.   40
First printing, September 2012

Book design by Aaron Zenz and Jennifer Rinaldi

the ChimpanSNEEZE

by Aaron Zenz

SCHOLASTIC INC.

A chimpanzee and a kinkajou
took a walk one day through the wild.
The kinkajou spotted buttercups,
so he plucked them up and smiled.

The chimpanzee sniffed the big bouquet,
but the buttercups made her wheeze.

Then the kinkajou flew into the blue . . .
all because of the **CHIMPANSNEEZE**.

The kinkajou neared an elephant,
who was painting a purple gate.
"Look out below!" yelled the kinkajou,
but he shouted a bit too late.

The kinkajou
hit the elephant
after falling
through the trees.

Now her head is stuck
in the **ELEFENCE** . . .

all because of
the **CHIMPANSNEEZE**.

A buffalo left a bakery
carrying little loaves of bread.

He planned to feed bitty birds with them,
but he tripped on a trunk instead.

the elefence

Now tumbling ryes
of varied size
are the only things
he sees.

For he's dropped
every single **BUFFALOAF** . . .

all because of
the **CHIMPANSNEEZE**.

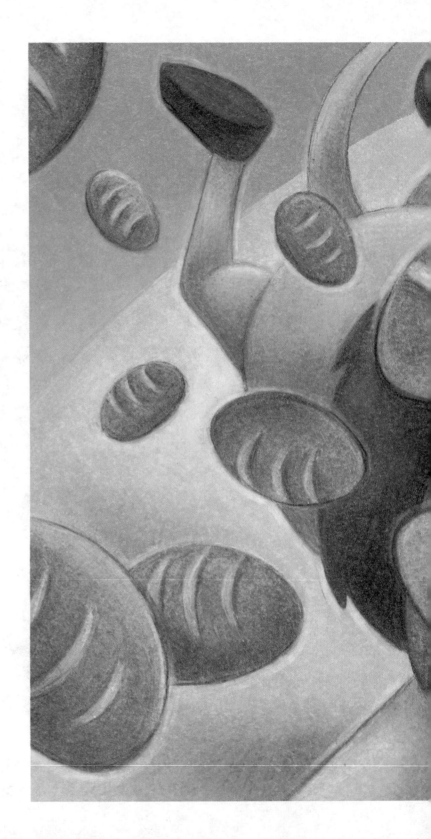

A hippo withdrew from a barbecue
with a hamburger for his trip.
He rolled on loaves from the buffalo,
and the mustard flew from his grip.

The accident
made him somersault,
and a yellow ~~fount~~ *mustard bottle*
was squeezed.

Now he's
HIPPOPOTAMUSTARD-
topped . . .

all because of
the **CHIMPANSNEEZE**.

A poodle pup left the beauty shop
with a dazzling new hairdo.

She slipped in the slop
of the hippopot'
and she fumbled
her pink shampoo.

The poodle pup
tossed her bottles up,
and the bubbles flew
where they pleased.

Now she's swimming amid
SHAMPOODLE suds . . .

all because of
the **CHIMPANSNEEZE**.

The kinkajou hunted high and low,
and he just couldn't find his friend.

Chimpy...
where are
you?

But bubbles popped
and his nose itchy-twitched
as a sneeze came on, there and then.

Pop!

Ah...

Ahh...

First a gasp of air,
then a thunderous sound,
and a wondrous, wild wind blew.

Chimpy!

And he landed back with the chimpanzee . . .
all because of his **KINKACHOO**!

Elefence   buffaloaf   hippomustas   shampoodle

chimpanzee   kinkajou

Did You Know . . .

Fifty-three chimps auditioned for the lead role in *The Chimpansneeze*. The part ultimately was awarded to rising chimp star Louise McGillicuddy, who beat out such notable performers as "Bim-Bim," "Chee-Chee," and "Mr. Nanners."

 Many of the wire harnesses used for the flying and falling stunts in this book are the very same ones employed in the making of *Peter Pan*—another role that, coincidentally, when not played by a woman, is often played by a kinkajou instead.

Special care was taken not to waste the food products used in the making of *The Chimpansneeze*. After each take, the hippo was shuttled to a shelter for wayward kittens and licked clean.

 The elephant's "Purple Gate" is now part of the permanent collection of Meeza Port's Prop Museum. You can see the famous gate on display Monday through Friday, showcased between Citizen Kane's sled and the Stinky Cheese Man's lips.

For this book, the character of the buffalo was created digitally by a team of 215 technicians. For reference, his actions were masterfully performed by Andy Serkis, who wore a makeshift motion-capture suit constructed out of marshmallows and duct tape.

 The shampoo used by the poodle was apple-scented. During rehearsals, the smell attracted horses from three neighboring counties.